the **BAD GUYS**

in

THE ONE?!

TEXT AND ILLUSTRATIONS COPYRIGHT © 2020 BY AARON BLABEY

ALL RIGHTS RESERVED. PUBLISHED BY SCHOLASTIC INC., *PUBLISHERS SINCE 1920*, SCHOLASTIC AND ASSOCIATED LOGOS ARE TRADEMARKS AND/OR REGISTERED TRADEMARKS OF SCHOLASTIC INC. THIS EDITION PUBLISHED UNDER LICENSE FROM SCHOLASTIC AUSTRALIA PTY LIMITED. FIRST PUBLISHED BY SCHOLASTIC AUSTRALIA PTY LIMITED IN 2020.

THE PUBLISHER DOES NOT HAVE ANY CONTROL OVER AND DOES NOT ASSUME ANY RESPONSIBILITY FOR AUTHOR OR THIRD-PARTY WEBSITES OR THEIR CONTENT.

NO PART OF THIS PUBLICATION MAY BE REPRODUCED, STORED IN A RETRIEVAL SYSTEM, OR TRANSMITTED IN ANY FORM OR BY ANY MEANS, ELECTRONIC, MECHANICAL, PHOTOCOPYING, RECORDING, OR OTHERWISE, WITHOUT WRITTEN PERMISSION OF THE PUBLISHER. FOR INFORMATION REGARDING PERMISSION, WRITE TO SCHOLASTIC AUSTRALIA, AN IMPRINT OF SCHOLASTIC AUSTRALIA PTY LIMITED, 345 PACIFIC HIGHWAY, LINDFIELD NSW 2070 AUSTRALIA.

THIS BOOK IS A WORK OF FICTION. NAMES, CHARACTERS, PLACES, AND INCIDENTS ARE EITHER THE PRODUCT OF THE AUTHOR'S IMAGINATION OR ARE USED FICTITIOUSLY, AND ANY RESEMBLANCE TO ACTUAL PERSONS, LIVING OR DEAD, BUSINESS ESTABLISHMENTS, EVENTS, OR LOCALES IS ENTIRELY COINCIDENTAL.

ISBN 978-1-338-32950-6

1 2020

PRINTED IN THE U.S.A.
FIRST U.S. PRINTING 2020

· AARON BLABEY ·

the **BAD GUYS**

in

THE ONE?!

SCHOLASTIC INC.

GASP!

DON'T LIE. I KNOW ALL.
YOU SAW A PATHETIC, POWERLESS CREATURE, HATED AND FEARED...

THAT'S ALWAYS BEEN YOUR NIGHTMARE HASN'T IT?

Yes . . .
but then Wolf . . .

THE WOLF HASN'T CHANGED ANYTHING!

THE WORLD STILL SEES YOU AS A LOATHSOME SNAKE.

BUT LET ME TELL YOU A SECRET.

YOU SHOULDN'T FEAR NIGHTMARES.

YOU ARE THE NIGHTMARE.

Are you really here?
Or are you just in my mind?
Where are you, exactly?

I'M **EXACTLY** WHERE I NEED TO BE, AND **SO ARE YOU.** YOU ARE FINALLY AMONG **TRUE FRIENDS.** YOU SHALL TAKE YOUR **RIGHTFUL** PLACE **HERE** AMONG MY

UNDERLORDS.

AND YOU WILL HELP US
SNUFF OUT OUR FINAL ENEMY,
THE CREATURE THEY CALL...

· CHAPTER 1 ·
THE ONE
PART ONE

OK,
SUDDENLY SUPER FOX...
You have some major
explaining to do.

But first,

YOU!

START TALKING!

What's going on with Snake?!

And how did he make us all turn . . .

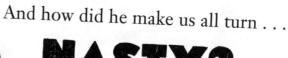

NASTY?

Hmm . . . look, I'm not *entirely* sure,

but I think Mr. Snake has got himself some

EXTRA superpowers by opening the

LAST REMAINING DOORWAY

into the # MULTIVERSE.

And, yeah, that's

. . . not great.

Oooh, a doorway into the

MULTIVERSE.

How interesting . . .

OK, I'll be the idiot—what's a **MULTIVERSE?**

It's **MULTIPLE UNIVERSES,** existing *side by side* . . .

Well, it's a bit more complicated than *that* . . .

Perhaps Nathan could explain it with a **REALLY SIMPLE DIAGRAM,** because I think anyone who doesn't understand THIS concept will be **COMPLETELY LOST** from this point on.

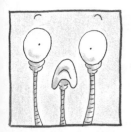

SURE.
No pressure, then . . .

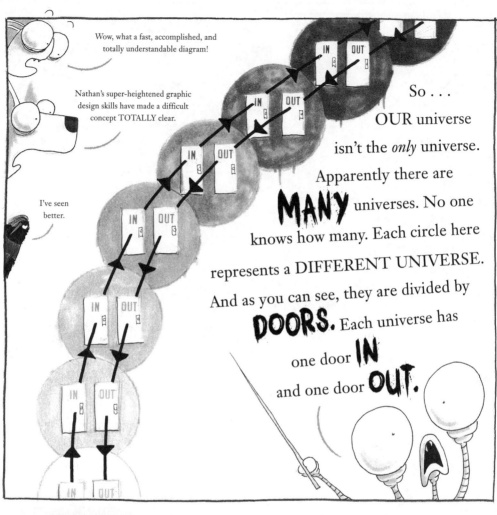

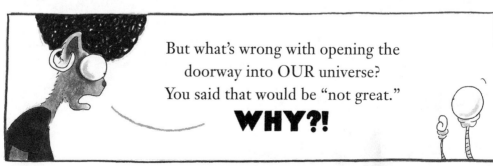

Well, legend has it that the ENTIRE MULTIVERSE is ruled by an **EVIL CENTIPEDE-LOOKIN' DUDE.** He's, like, REALLY bad news. **BUT!** OUR little universe has always been **SAFE** from him because he's never been able to find the DOORWAY **IN** ...

Until now.

Yep.

But how do you *KNOW THIS*?

If this CENTIPEDE thing has never been able to enter OUR universe, *how do you even* *KNOW HE EXISTS?*

Ah, well, that's a funny story . . .
Do you guys remember **PRINCE MARMALADE?**

Uh-huh.

Yeah, well, his *dad—***THE KING***—*
was drag racing his space cruiser one day,
a loooooooong time ago, when he saw a
WORMHOLE, right?

Uh-huh.

But it didn't look like a normal wormhole. It had, like,

FREAKY STUFF

coming out of it . . .

Freaky stuff?

Yeah! But when he tried to suck the **FREAKY STUFF** into his cruiser's power core— *just to see what would happen, you know?*—it, uh . . .

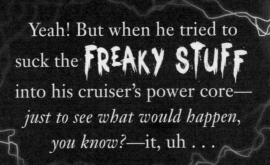

Uh-huh?

It kind of . . .

FREAKED OUT!

Freaked out?

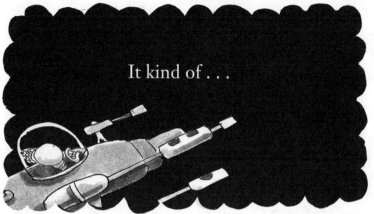

Yeah! And it didn't just freak out *his* ship. It caused a chain reaction that infected **ALL** of our technology. Kind of like a computer virus. Only *freakier* . . .

Uh-huh.

And **SUDDENLY** all of *our cannons and transports and stuff* had all these

WEIRD NEW POWERS,

which would have been totally sweet, buuuuuut —spoiler alert— when the cruiser freaked out, the king had . . .

A VISION!

A vision?

A vision of a giant **CENTIPEDE-LOOKIN' DUDE.** He wanted us to **USE** those powers, because according to the king's vision, they would **RIP OPEN THE DOORWAY TO OUR UNIVERSE.** THEN the **CENTIPEDE-LOOKIN' DUDE** and all his other evil **DUDEROONIES** would be able to come busting in and, like, **DESTROY ALL LIVING THINGS.**

I know, right?

THEN **WHY** _DID YOU COME TO EARTH_ **BLASTING THOSE CANNONS** _EVERY FIVE MINUTES IF YOU_ _KNEW_ _IT WOULD RIP OPEN THE DOORWAY?_ _AND_ **WHY** _DID YOU LET US USE THOSE_ **ESCAPE PODS** _BACK IN_ **BOOK SIX?!**

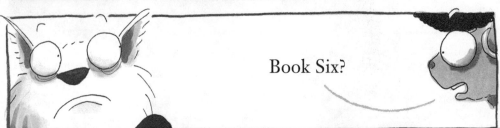

Book Six?

You know—it's like if our life was some kind of *series*, then that part *probably* would have happened around Book Six . . .

Maybe around page 122 . . .

Let's move on, shall we?

SO WHY DID YOU LET US?!

He didn't **TELL US** it was dangerous!
He only told Marmalade!
And *Marmalade* forgot!

So what can we do?

Oh. Nothing.
WE'RE ALL GOING TO DIE.

THAT'S how you're going to deliver that piece of information?

Oh, yeah, sorry . . .
But there's **NOTHING**
that can stop him now.
There's—

THERE IS ONE

WHO CAN STOP HIM!

AGAIN *WITH THE EYES AND THE FLOATING?!*

WHAT is going on with

PIRANHA?!

THERE IS ONE
CHANCE!

ONE!

What chance?

Not *WHAT!*
WHO!

ONE!

FAAAAAAART!

SPLAT!

That *smell* again!
WHERE does it come from?!

Piranha!
What did you mean?!
Who is . . .
THE ONE?

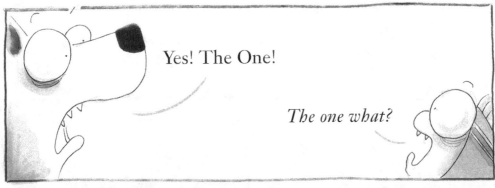

What a mystery.

I wonder . . .
who could it be . . .

Kitty, there's something I've been meaning to—

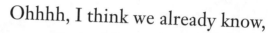

Ohhhh, I think we already know, DON'T WE?! Our fearless leader and **TRUSTED FRIEND** has a WHOLE **SECRET LIFE** she never *felt* like telling us about, doesn't she?!

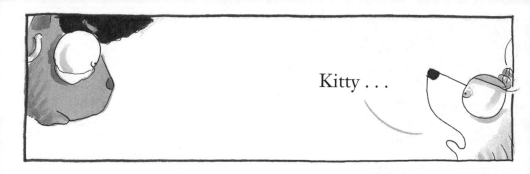

Kitty . . .

So when some **INTERDIMENSIONAL SUPER-DEMON**
suddenly bursts into our world, *SHE* is the only one who can

whip out *magical powers* to slow it down.

MAGICAL FORCE-FIELDY STUFF—

shooting out of her hands like a WIZARD!—
that she's never thought to mention before!

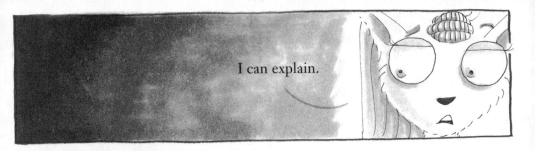

I don't care about
your explanation!
I just want the TRUTH.
Is it true?

Are you . . .
THE ONE?

Yes.

Hang on, what does
that even mean?!

The One *what?*

WHO CARES?!

It's *VERY* nice to meet you,
LITTLE MISS ONE.

You look just like a friend
I *THOUGHT* I knew.

Kitty, baby . .

I'm out.

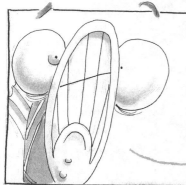

Chicos, *I'm confused.*
Last thing I remember, I was
SHAKING MY BOOTY, but now
the party vibes have gone out.
Who killed my vibe?!

· CHAPTER 2 ·

ONSLAUGHT

Is that . . .
*HEAVY METAL
GUITAR?!*

Yes. I can do this.

WE HAVE A **NEW** UNDERLORD AMONG US. IF HE BELIEVES HE CAN **TURN** THESE HOPELESS CREATURES INTO OUR ALLIES, THEN LET HIM **TRY**. WHAT HARM CAN IT DO?

REMEMBER, **YOU** WEREN'T ALWAYS AS **POWERFUL** AS YOU ARE **NOW.**

DARK LORD OF SERPENTS. SEDUCE YOUR FRIENDS AND BRING ME THE ONE.

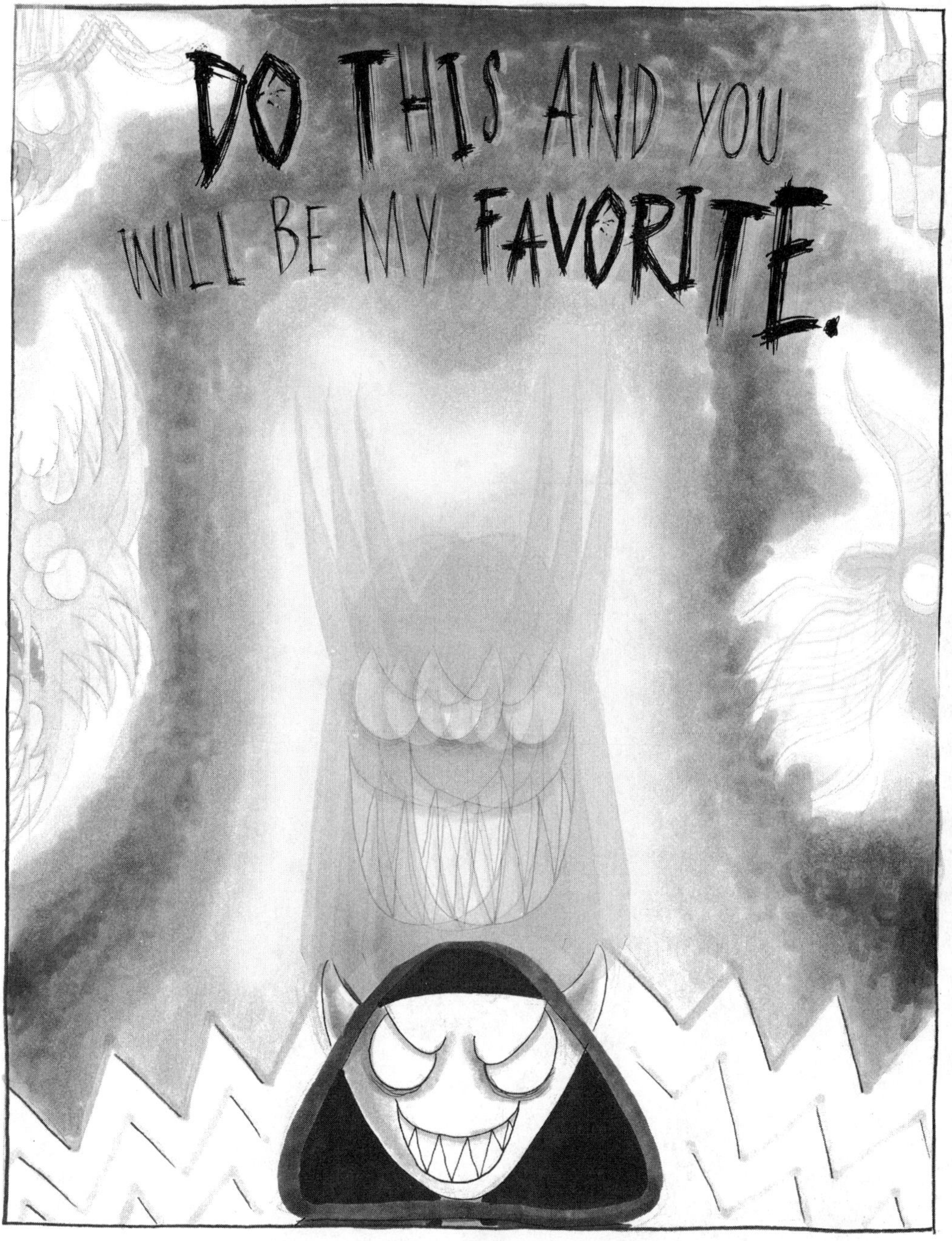
DO THIS AND YOU WILL BE MY FAVORITE.

DIDDY WIDDLY!
DIDDY WIDDLY!
DIDDY WIDDLY!
SQUEEEAL!
KA-CHUGGADACHUGADACHUGADADA

· CHAPTER 3 ·
THE ONE
PART TWO

So . . . you're The One?

'Fraid so.

And again, what does that *mean* exactly?

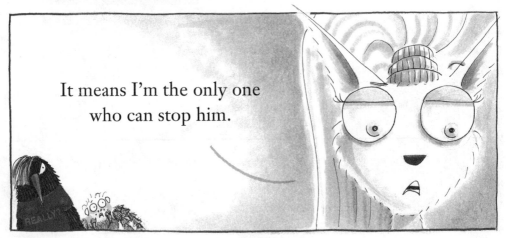

It means I'm the only one who can stop him.

WHO?

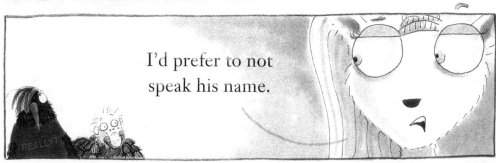

I'd prefer to not speak his name.

Really?
He-really-shall-not-be-named?
Really?!

OK, sure.
He's called . . .

DIDDY WIDDLY!
DIDDY WIDDLY!
DIDDY WIDDLY!
SQUEEEAL!
DREAD OVERLORD
SPLAARGHÖN
KA-CHUGGADACHUGADACHUGADA

Was that *heavy metal guitar?!*

Yessss, it happens when you **SAY HIS NAME.** It can't be helped.

That's kind of awesome . . .

Give me *punk*, any day . . .

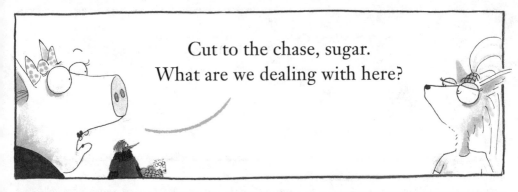

Cut to the chase, sugar.
What are we dealing with here?

He's the
END OF ALL LIFE.
No question about it.
And **I'M** the only creature in the
MULTIVERSE that can stop him.

But why *YOU?*

I'm sorry but that's
all I can tell you . . . for now.

DUDE, I've heard stories about

THE SPLÄARGHÖN

DIDDY WIDDLY! *DIDDY WIDDLY!*
DIDDY WIDDLY! **SQUEEEAL!**

KA-CHUGGADA CHUGADACHUGADA

and my advice to you is RUN!
If you really are a **THREAT** to him, he will
summon every **EVIL FORCE**
in the MULTIVERSE and aim
them directly at **YOU!**

Good grief! He's right!
We must find somewhere
to **HIDE** you!

Sorry, Milt, but it doesn't work that way.
He'll send his forces for me,
but **HE'S** a coward.
HE'LL hide as far from me as he can.
THAT means I have to find
EVERY SINGLE DOORWAY
between **ME AND HIM** and
CROSS THE ENTIRE MULTIVERSE
to get to him.

So, as nice as it would be
to run away from all this . . .
I have no choice.

I have to go straight *toward* it . . .

into the heart of darkness.

Trouble is . . .
I don't know where
those doorways are.

Not even the first one.

Huh?

What do you mean?
The first doorway is

OVER THERE!

Snake opened it *right here*
in the building.

No, remember Nathan's
excellent diagram?
That's just
the doorway

INTO

our world.

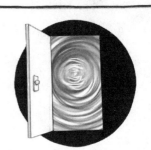

We have to find the doorway **OUT.**

But no one knows where that is . . .

37!

56!

55!

98!

OK! THAT'S IT!
WHAT'S GOING ON
WITH THE
PIRANHA?!

He's no longer
MR. PIRANHA.
He's become . . .

145! *26!* *26!* *59!*

THE ORACLE!

He's *what?!*

I don't have time to explain.
I *will*, but not now . . .

Hey! Those
NUMBERS!
I know what they are! They're—

MAP COORDINATES!

He's giving us directions to the
FIRST DOORWAY!

He's *WHAT?!*

HOW?!

How does the piranha
suddenly know where the
DOORWAY is?!

43!
39!
79!
25!

Piranha doesn't.
But he's **CHANNELING**
someone who *does*.
There's . . . **SOMEONE** . . .
helping us.
Piranha is just the vessel.

Is someone writing
these numbers down?

I've got it!
I've got the **LOCATION.**
It's only a few miles from here.
What are the chances . . .

That's not a coincidence.

Wait!
Someone's helping us?
Who?
Who's helping us?!

Do you trust me?

Well, totally, yes.

Then trust me now.
We need to *leave here*.
RIGHT NOW.

4536281!

23678!

674522!

2579!

258947472!

My goodness!
MORE coordinates!
These ones are . . . a little
FARTHER AWAY...

How much farther?

92 MILLION
LIGHT-YEARS away.

What?! *WHY?!*

HIDDEN REALM!
THE OTHERS!
THE ONE WILL FAIL!
THE
HEED MY WORD!
FAAAAAARRT!

Man, is he going to fart
EVERY time he has a

VISION?

*Fishin'?
Who's going fishin'?
I'll bite their arms off!*

This is what I was afraid of . . .

THIS *is what you were afraid of?!*

It's my **DESTINY** to **FIND THE DOORWAYS** and journey through **THE MULTIVERSE . . .**

HOW
DO YOU
KNOW
THAT?!

. . . but someone else
needs to look for the

HIDDEN REALM

and locate

THE OTHERS.

I'm guessing the
HIDDEN REALM
is at the *other* location . . .

The good news is—
that's here in **OUR** universe!

The bad news is—it's
**92 MILLION
LIGHT-YEARS**
away . . .

Well, that's not **TOTALLY** bad news . . .

The message said,
"A **HERO** *must go to the Hidden Realm*,"
not
"A **BUTT-HANDED WEIRDO**
must go . . ."

Joy!

Hey!

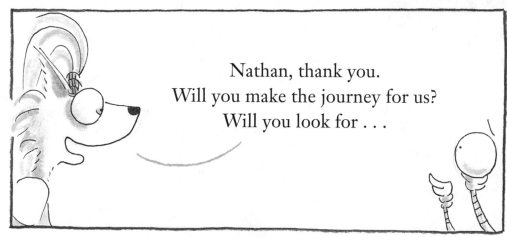

Nathan, thank you.
Will you make the journey for us?
Will you look for . . .

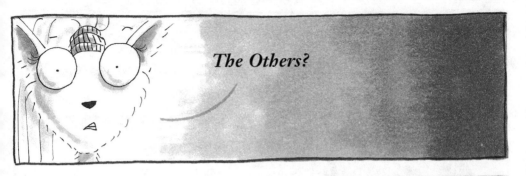

The Others?

Sure. Why not?

Sorry to
be a pest . . .
*but who are
The Others?!*

Still trust me?

Totally, yes, 100%.

Then trust me on that, too.

But I guess we don't really
have a choice.

And I mean **RIGHT NOW!**

KA-BOOM!

KA-BOOM!

This story is getting VERY exciting, isn't it?

TIFFANY FLUFFIT LIVE! 6 NEWS

CHAPTER 4
THE GREAT DIVIDE

OW! I'M STUCK!

My wing's caught on your ridiculous

SELF-BALANCING
PERSONAL
TRANSPORTER.

Why do you need this?!
You're the fastest biped
on the planet!

That's OK.
We can all just go with

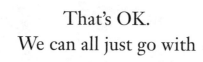

NATHAN and help him find

THE OTHERS . . .

WHAT?!

NOOOOOOOO!

Wait, *I'm stuck!*

There's CLEARLY an

A-TEAM AND B-TEAM

thing happening here.

By which, I mean—

you're the **A-TEAM**

standing over there

looking all heroic . . .

While I'm trapped over here with a bunch of **ODDBALLS** and **WEIRDOS** who will evidently be making up the **B-TEAM! DOES THIS LOOK LIKE THE MAIN CAST TO YOU?!**

Ahhhh-choo!

My hand cream!

My asthma inhaler!

Wait! My heart pills!

I REFUSE TO GET *TRAPPED IN A* **LESS IMPORTANT SUBPLOT!**

I disagree! I think **OUR** plot could potentially be the most **EXCITING ONE!**

Wake up, man! WE'RE **SECOND BANANAS,** AT BEST!

I sure will.

NO HEROICS FROM YOU!

YOU are **THE ONE** and you have **ONE** job— get to the

EVIL HEAVY METAL DUDE

on the other side of the **MULTIVERSE.**

WE have one job— **STOP YOU FROM GETTING KILLED** before you get there.

Got it?

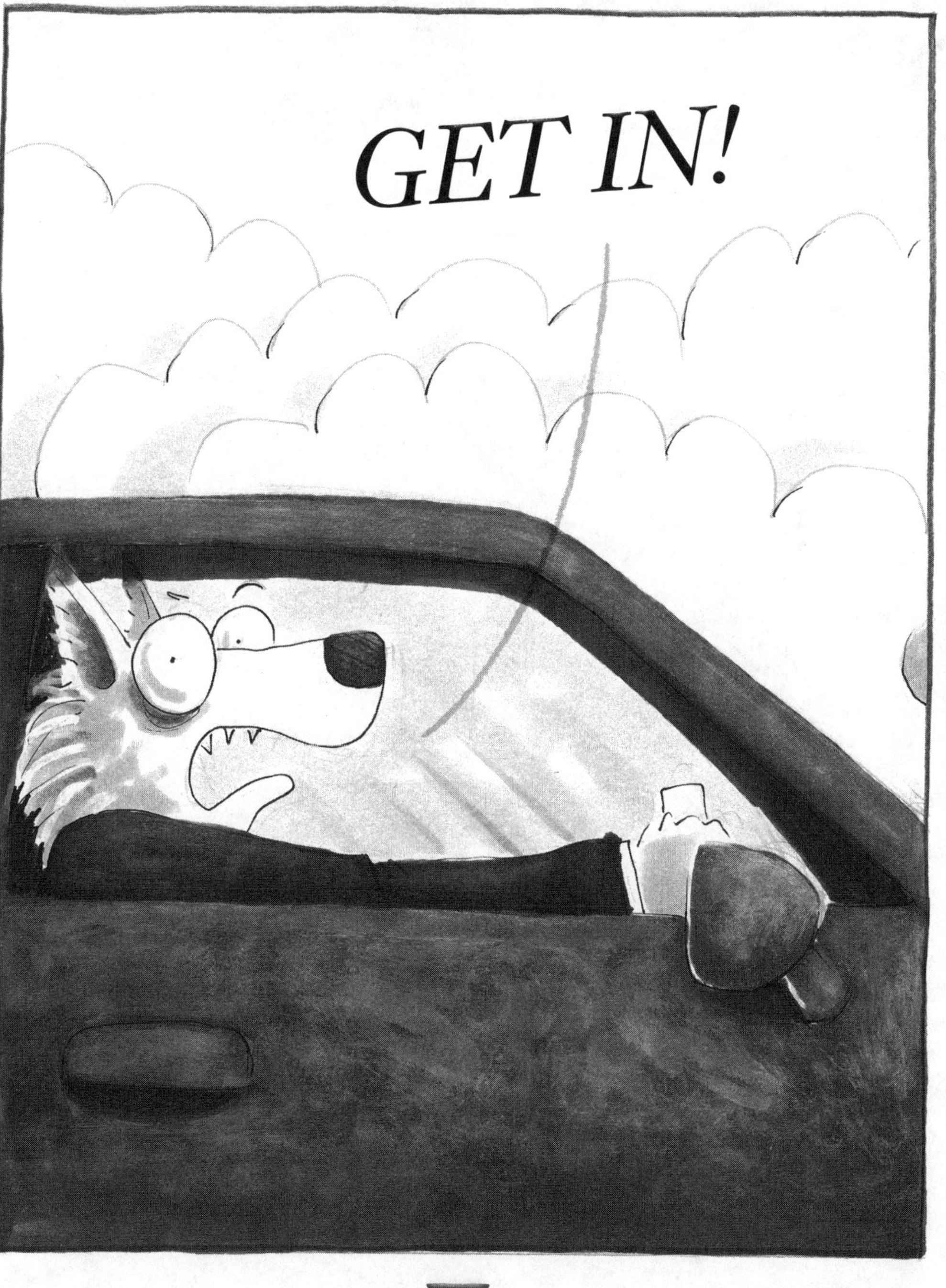
GET IN!

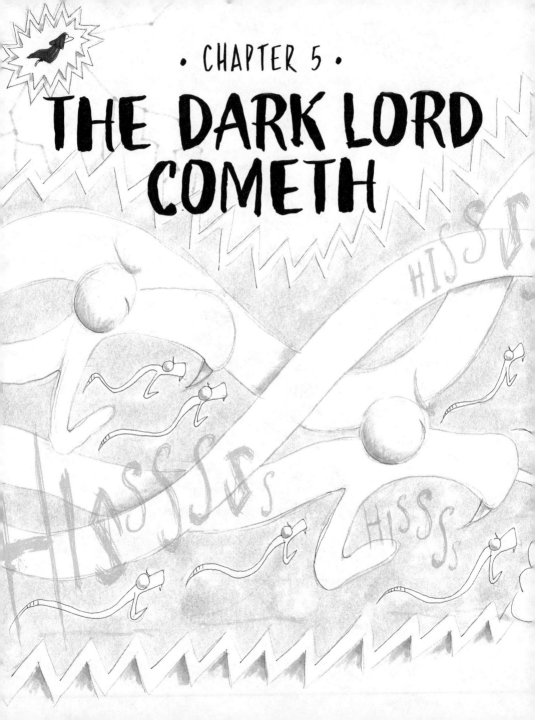

· CHAPTER 5 ·

THE DARK LORD COMETH

I have to get out of here. I'm **ENDANGERING** all of you!

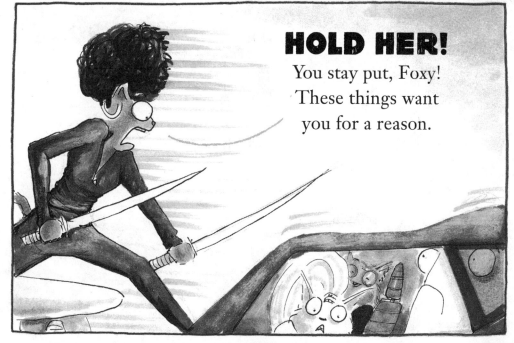

HOLD HER! You stay put, Foxy! These things want you for a reason.

We have to keep you safe, baby.

Sharky, sit on her, will you?

What?!

You got it.

Wait! Gah!

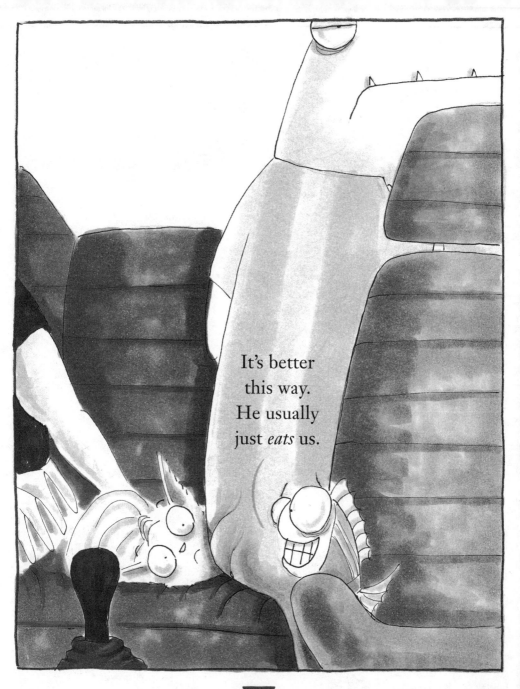

These idiots are going to get themselves killed.

STOP RUNNING!

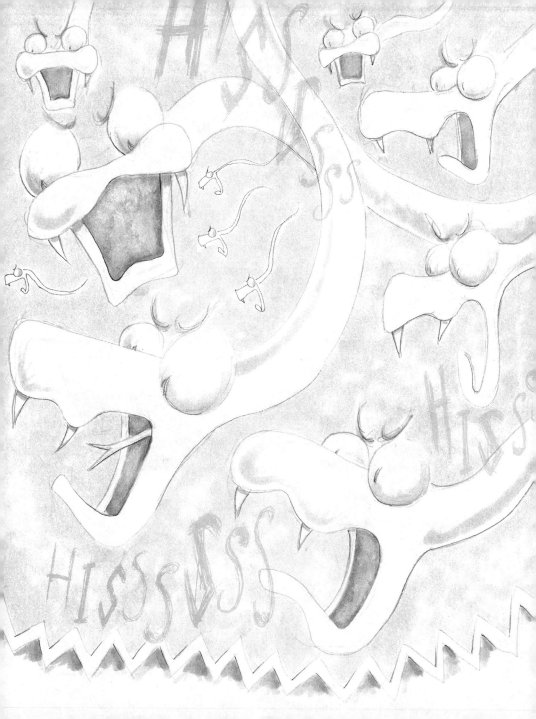

Ohhhhhhh . . .
that's *awesome* . . .

GIVE IN TO IT.

Yessssss . . .

BRAAAAKE!

Wha . . . ?
What happened?

You started acting **WEIRD,** *chico*!

Like YOU can talk, *MR. ORACLE!*

It always has to be the

HARD WAY.

OK . . .

HERE, KITTY KITTY KITTY!

Huh?

Untrustworthy?!
Just because you're **PERFECT**
all the time.

· CHAPTER 6 ·
THE B-TEAM

See?!

This group is so **UNCOOL,** no one's even bothered to chase us!

I don't think that's the reason. We're . . . cool . . .

I think you're cool! I really do!

That's like his **MOTHER** telling him he's cool! It doesn't count!

Hmmm, yeah, guys . . . it's been *great* . . .
but since it's calmed down a little bit,
I think I might see if I can hook up
with the coole*rrrr* . . . I mean . . .
OTHER team.
Yeah.
But thanks a bunch, though . . .

That's *cold*.
Cold as ice.

Wait up!
Dinosaur Nerd!
Unhook me from this stupid thing!

GOSSIP GIRL!

I'm coming with you!

I'm an *award-winning journalist!*

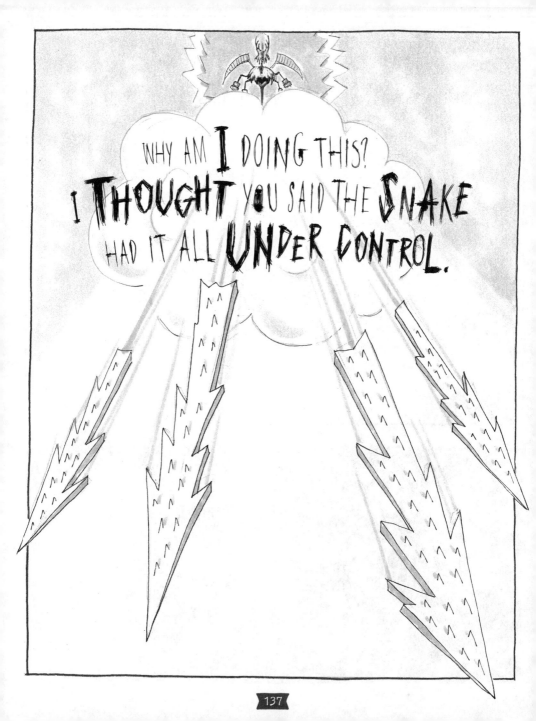

· CHAPTER 7 ·
SHOWDOWN

NO!

FOX, YOU'RE MAKING A MISTAKE!

GIVE. IN. TO. IT.

IT'S AWESOME!

UUUURRRRGGGHHH!

I'm sorry?
Your *what?*

Buddy . . .
please wake up.

I CAN'T HOLD HIM MUCH LONGER . . .

GET . . . IN . . . THE CAR . . .

Buddy?

WHAT ARE YOU WAITING FOR?!

It's **HER.**
She's too strong.

· CHAPTER 8 ·

DOORWAY #1

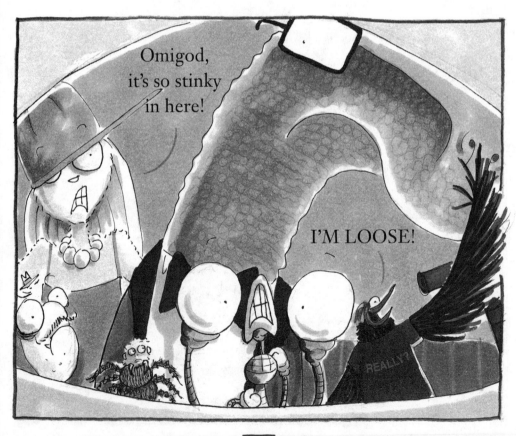

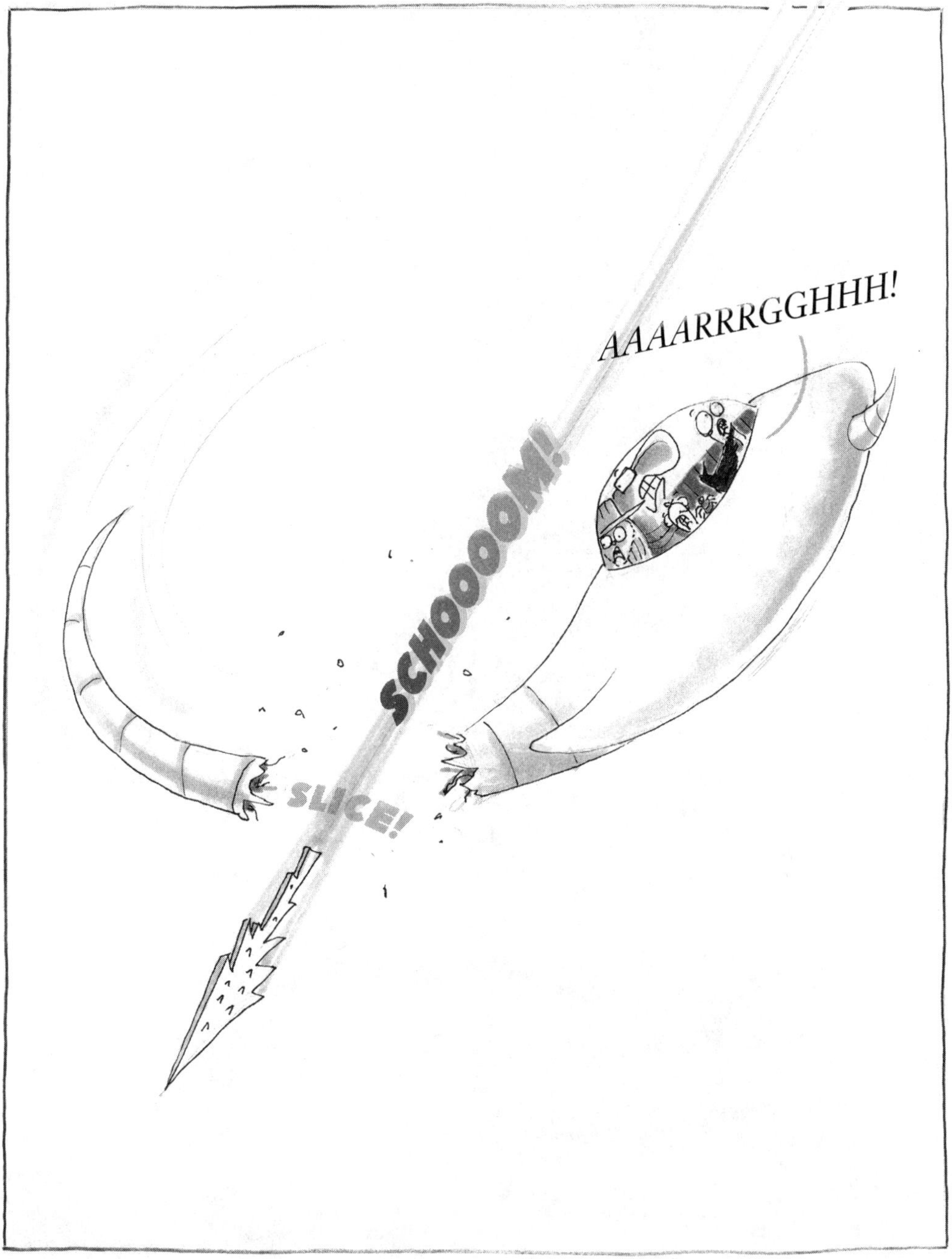
AAAARRRGGHHH!
SCHOOOOM!
SLICE!

Piranha, are we nearly there?! Where is this

DOORWAY

supposed to be?

The **GPS** says it's just up ahead . . .
but I've been wondering . . .

If this doorway leads to

ANOTHER UNIVERSE . . .

how come *no one has discovered it before?*

Maybe it's hidden?

DISGUISED

as something else?

*Chico!* This doorway could be
MILLIONS OF YEARS OLD!
What could you possibly
**DISGUISE IT AS**
to keep everyone away from it for
THAT LONG?

That'd probably do it . . .

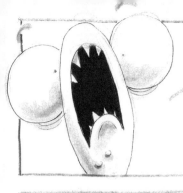

POOP BURGERS!?

Wait a minute.
GRANNY GUMBO'S POOP BURGERS?!

GRANNY GUMBO?!
I remember her . . .

If our life *was* a series,
she'd probably have appeared in
BOOK 4 . . .
or something.

OK, that's starting to
get on my nerves.

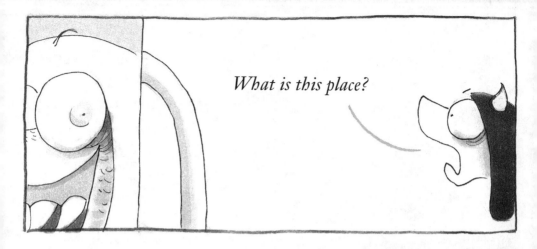

What is this place?

Something you don't fully understand.

I'm sorry about this, Mr. Snake . . .

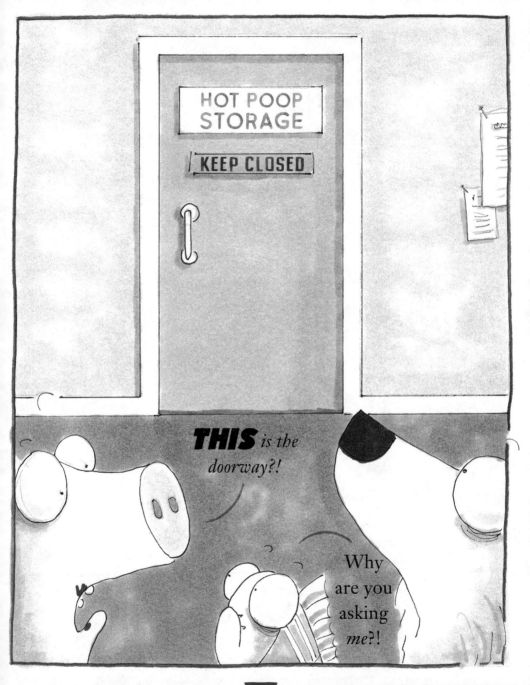

· CHAPTER 9 ·

HOT POOP

I don't understand . . .

I don't know what happened! *I did turn them!* **A few times!** But SHE kept getting in the way.

ENOUGH. IT'S TIME TO LEARN FROM A MORE EXPERIENCED UNDERLORD.

SCRAAAAAAPE...

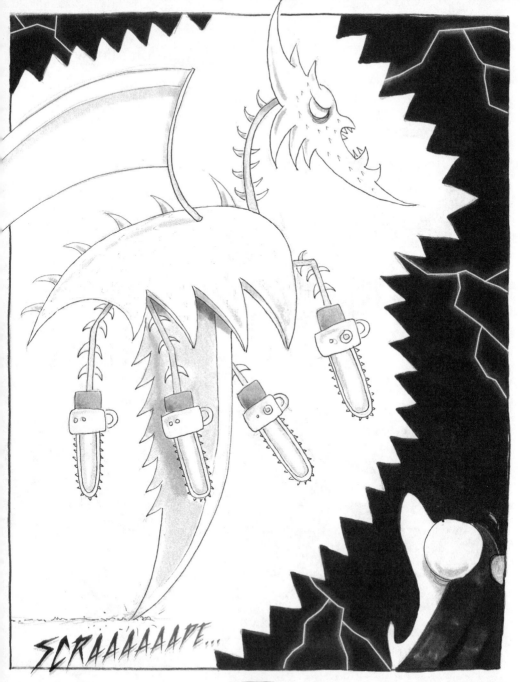

SCRAAÄÄAAAPE...

GET OUT OF MY WAY, SNAKE.
THEY'RE IN MY UNIVERSE NOW.
I WILL DESTROY THE ONE.
HOT PO
STORA
KEEP CL

SO TO BE CLEAR—

TEAM A HAS GONE THROUGH A **DOOR** IN A **POOP RESTAURANT** TO FIND AN **EVIL CENTIPEDE** IN A **DISTANT UNIVERSE,** WHILE **TEAM B** IS SPINNING ITS WAY ACROSS THE GALAXY TO FIND SOME DUDES CALLED **THE OTHERS** WHO ARE, APPARENTLY, **REALLY** IMPORTANT, BUT **THE ONE** **(AKA AGENT FOX)** IS BEING **REALLY** VAGUE ABOUT **WHY** THEY'RE IMPORTANT.

GOT IT? **GOOD.** *SO EVERYONE'S HAPPY?*

NO! NOT HAPPY!
I'M ON THE WRONG TEEEEEEEEEAAAAAAAM!!!

the **BAD GUYS**
BOOK 13!

COMING SOON...